The Sugar Creek Mystery

Andy Gonzalez

declared or implied. Readers acknowledge that the author is not engaged in the rendering of legal, financial, medical or professional advice. The content within this book has been derived from various sources. Please consult a licensed professional before attempting any techniques outlined in this book.

By reading this document, the reader agrees that under no circumstances is the author responsible for any losses, direct or indirect, that are incurred as a result of the use of the information contained within this document, including, but not limited to, errors, omissions, or inaccuracies.

CONTENTS

CHAPTER 1

Life at Tall Oaks

Life at the Tall Oaks trailer park in Sugar Creek Township, Indiana can be a little rough and tumble at times. For some folks, it's the end of the line. For others, it's a chance at a fresh start. Others are drifters and just passing through. If there's one thing that all of the residents share in common, it's that they're quite the colorful cast of characters. As a result, there's never a dull moment at Tall Oaks.

It's a place that's garnered a reputation for getting loud, rowdy, and at times even a little dangerous. The local sheriff, Arnold Perkins, and his officers have been out to the trailer park on several occasions for various disturbances and fights. These types of occurrences are commonplace because some of the residents in the trailer park love to let the liquor flow like the Wabash River, which flows and winds its way through Sugar Creek.

The town of Sugar Creek is surrounded by hectares of lush, thriving forests. A place known as the Rocky Hollow Falls Canyon Nature Preserve. This vast expanse is where Wyatt Jenkins escapes when life in the trailer park becomes difficult or, unfortunately, unbearable. Wyatt is a shy, quiet boy and despite only having had twelve trips around the sun, has grown up fast. He has seen and been through a lot in his short time on Earth.

It's late June, and Wyatt has just completed his final day of the seventh grade. Summer break has arrived and he hopes that the next few months will be filled with at least a modicum of excitement and adventure. Little does he know, he's about to get a lot more than he bargained for.

A yellow school bus pulls up to the trailer park, stops, and the driver opens the lone side door. Wyatt steps off the bus with his school bag slung over his shoulders. He wears shorts and a shirt with an image of a bald eagle on it. It's a scorching day and beads of sweat cover Wyatt's forehead.

Wyatt's relieved to see that a blue Ford pick-up truck isn't parked next to his trailer. That means his mother's on and off again boyfriend, Hank, isn't there. Wyatt thinks to himself, *Thank*

God that douchebag isn't there. A quiet night with my mom would be great.

As Wyatt approaches his trailer, a chubby man driving a riding lawn mower approaches him. This is Mr. Stevens, the trailer park superintendent. Despite having familial relation to Hank, one could say that Mr. Stevens was cut from the same cloth.

"Where's your ma, is she home?" asks Mr. Stevens. "I need that goddamn rent money." he grumbles rudely to the boy.

"I-" says Wyatt when suddenly the trailer door swings open and Emily storms out. "Are you kidding me?! Don't you *ever* talk to my son like that again!"

"Now, you listen here, Emily! I've been more than patient with you, you know how much the upkeep on this park costs?" shouts Mr. Stevens as Wyatt runs past Emily into the trailer slamming the door.

"Oh please, upkeep for what?! This is the first time I've seen you cut the grass in months! It's two feet high! I've had it with your fat ass, Donald!" yells Emily.

"Don't call me Donald, it's Mr. Stevens, and if you're not happy living here Emily then move yourself and that little delinquent of yours outta my park!" asserts Mr. Stevens.

"I'll have a few hundred bucks for you by Friday, and don't you *ever* speak to my son like that again or call him a delinquent I swear to God. He's a good boy, he's never been in any kinda trouble. How many DUI's does your son Ronnie have again? Seven or is it nine now?

5

Everybody knows about that one, Donald." scolds Emily as she storms back into her trailer.

"I want the whole thing on Friday and don't you be talking about Ronnie!" hollers Mr. Stevens.

"Screw you, Donald. You'll get what I can give ya." she replies as she slams the door.

"This is what I get for rentin' to welfare cases. Serves me right." grumbles Mr. Stevens as he shifts the riding lawn more into gear and drives off.

Inside the trailer, Wyatt sits in the living room. He watches a wildlife show about common animals found in Brazil's Amazon rainforest. This particular segment features one of the Amazon's most elusive predators, the jaguar.

Emily approaches and sighs, frustrated.

She plops down on the couch next to Wyatt, smiles, and puts a loving arm around him.

"I love you." she says.

"Love you too, mom."

"What're you watchin'?" asks Emily.

"Some show about jaguars."

"Where're they? Africa?" inquires Emily.

"No, Brazil and other parts of South America."

"Are you hungry?" asks Emily.

"Yeah, a little."

"How bout some chicken fingers?" suggests Emily.

"Chicken fingers again, that's all I ever eat."

"Well, excuse me King Tut, but I haven't had a chance to get to the grocery store yet." admits Emily. "Hank said he'd take me tonight or tomorrow."

Wyatt grows angry and clenches his fists.

"I thought you were done with that douchebag, mom."

"Wyatt, don't call him that. He's all I got and that's better than nothing." argues Emily.

"But he's not better than nothing! *Nothing* would be better than Hank. I just finished the seventh grade and even I understand that but you can't?! He treats us like shit! He steps foot in this trailer again and I swear to God I'll run away and you'll *never* see me again!" warns Wyatt.

The comment hurts Emily and her eyes water. When she was Wyatt's age, she was what social services referred to as a "runner" because she ran from every single foster home she was ever sent to.

"Just answer me one thing?" says Wyatt.

"What's that?"

"How does it feel to know that you're dumber than an eighth grader?" quips Wyatt, receiving a quick reflex slap to the mouth.

"God, I hate you." says Wyatt calmly as he gets up from the couch and jogs to his room.

Emily breaks down in tears.

Wyatt enters his room and slams the door shut. He plops down on his bed and looks at a poster of the iconic comic book hero, Wolverine. He thinks to himself, *I wish I had huge muscles and razor-sharp steel claws that shot out of my hands because if I did, I'd pulverize Hank and rip him to shreds the next time he put a hand on me or my mom!*

Meanwhile, a blue Ford pick-up truck pulls into the trailer park and sure enough, it's Hank.

Hank drinks a can of warm beer as he drives toward Emily's trailer. He spots another woman of similar age walking along and scans her body with his eyes.

"Hey, hey what's cookin' good lookin'?" says Hank, sticking his head out the window.

"Ugh… in your dreams, Hank." replies the woman.

"Yes you are. At least three to four nights a week, baby." confesses Hank with a sleazy smile.

"Oh, really? Does Emily know that? Maybe I should let her know." inquires the woman, annoyed.

Hank's smile quickly fades.

"Alright, Norma Jean, bye now." says Hank as he steps on his fuel pedal and accelerates away.

Back in Wyatt's trailer, Emily lays on the couch and cries.

She hears the sound of a squeaky storm door opening and Hank walks inside.

"Hellooo?" calls out Hank as he puts what's left of his six-pack in the fridge.

Hank opens a fresh beer and heads to the living room belching a few times on the way. He sees Emily wiping tears from her eyes.

"What happened? Mr. Stevens botherin' you again or was it the little freak?" asks Hank.

"Don't call him that." says Emily.

Hank steps closer to Emily, glares down at her, and intimidates her.

"Watch your damn mouth, woman. I'll call that little freak whatever I damn well please, Emily. Where is the little shitstain anyway?"

"He's in his room, just leave him alone, Hank." advises Emily.

Hank turns and heads to Wyatt's room.

"Hank, please just leave him alone!"

Hank barges into Wyatt's room.

"Get the hell outta my room!"

"Shut up. What'd d'you do to your mother, you little shitstain? Why's she cryin'?!" shouts Hank.

"Get the hell outta my room you, asshole!"

Hank grabs Wyatt by the scruff of his t-shirt.

"Why's she cryin' ya freak?! Answer me!" yells Hank, as Wyatt hits his forearms and tries to kick him.

Emily rushes in and tries to pull Hank off of Wyatt.

"Get off of him, Hank!" says Emily.

Hank spins around and pushes Emily hard against a wall.

"She was crying because I told her I'd run away if you stepped foot back in this trailer you, douchebag!"

Hank relents and lets go of Wyatt's shirt.

"Get out!"

Hank turns and walks out of Wyatt's room. Emily looks at Wyatt and feels terrible.

"I hate you! Get out!"

Emily complies with Wyatt's wishes and closes the door.

Wyatt cries hard.

In the living room, Emily scolds Hank.

"You need to stop putting your hands on us, Hank. You can't do that!"

Emily and Hank argue and shout at one another.

Wyatt can hear them and covers his ears. He thinks to himself, *this is it I've had it. I'm done with this crap. I can't take it anymore! Stop your crying, you're not a baby.*

Wyatt wipes his tears and springs from his bed.

He approaches his bedroom door with purpose and locks it.

He heads for his closet, opens the door, and a ton of camping and hiking gear packed ceiling-high falls out of the closet and on top of him.

Thankfully, Wyatt walks away from the avalanche of gear unscathed.

He focuses, thinks fast, and acts even quicker. *I have to gather everything I need because I'm never coming back.*

He grabs a military-style rucksack, a compact one-man tent, and a sleeping bag.

He secures the tent and sleeping bag to his rucksack and then finds a compass and flashlight.

Next, he finds a map of the Rocky Hollow Falls Canyon Nature Preserve and stuffs it into his rucksack.

Wyatt rummages through the mound of gear and finds a box containing 1000 wooden stick matches.

He thinks to himself, *I'll definitely need those,* and stuffs them into his rucksack.

Wyatt finds a small telescopic fishing pole, a tiny tackle box with lures, and packs them.

He packs some pairs of shorts, clean underwear, t-shirts, and a durable must-have pair of hiking shoes. He's angry and rams the items into his rucksack forcefully.

He retrieves a set of Swiss Army knives, batteries, and puts them in his rucksack too.

***

Nighttime, a few hours later…

Wyatt is all packed up. He unlocks and opens his bedroom door a quarter of an inch and peeks out into the living room.

He sees his mother and Hank asleep on the couch. There's several cans and bottles of beer on the coffee table.

Wyatt tip toes out of his room and into the kitchen.

He opens the cupboards and removes some canned goods, granola bars, and as many juice boxes as he can carry.

Wyatt heads back into his bedroom and crams the items into his rucksack.

Wyatt sneaks back out, goes to the bathroom, and takes bars of soap and a bottle of shampoo.

He walks back into his bedroom and approaches his bedroom window.

Wyatt opens the window, picks up his rucksack, and shoves it through his window.

He walks over to his bedroom door and locks it.

Wyatt's heart pounds as he makes his way through the window.

He tumbles down to the soft grass below and is quick to get back on his feet. He puts his rucksack on and heads north.

Despite the heavy weight from his pack weighing him down, Wyatt feels more at ease, at peace, and safe with each step that he takes toward his forest of solitude. There isn't a doubt in Wyatt's mind that he's made the right decision. He can't help but think, *This will be a fresh start. The beginning of a great adventure!*

CHAPTER 2

1600 Acres

The Rocky Hollow Falls Canyon nature preserve is an expanse of trails, streams, centuries old hemlock trees, mosses, and naturally occurring hydrangeas. The sheer number of various species of animals in the preserve is astounding. The list ranges from chipmunks and cottontail rabbits to muskrats, wild hogs, and even larger predators like mountain lions and black bears.

Under the cover of night, Wyatt walks down a familiar path illuminated only by his flashlight. He's nervous about being in the woods at night but he'd rather be out in the wild than anywhere near the trailer park and the stench of stale beer and cigarettes.

The trail twists and turns through the trees and then finally, Wyatt sees it. A small clearing of grass with a few mature ferns, the perfect spot to pitch his tent and settle down for the night.

Wyatt nestles his flashlight into the y-intersection of a tree trunk and branch and shines it at the small clearing.

He unpacks his one-man pop up tent, shakes it open, and spikes it into the ground.

Wyatt puts his rucksack inside the tent, closes the flap, and zips it up. He retrieves his flashlight from the tree and sets off to find some logs and small pieces of wood to use for kindling.

Shining his flashlight around in search of wood, Wyatt hears ominous sounds emerge from the forest. His heart palpitates. For the first time since he left the trailer, he feels uneasy and although he'd never admit it, a little scared. He hears leaves rustle to the east, branches snapping and cracking from the north. Wyatt thinks, *Oh, crap, oh crap, what was that? Stop it. You have to be calm. You're the master of your environment. I am the master of my environment. This is my sixteen-hundred acre kingdom. I have every right to be here. As much as the animals do. I am the master of my environment, I am the master of my environment,* he reassures himself.

An owl hoots from the west and Wyatt spins around, shining the beam of his flashlight at the creature. The owl sits perched atop a tree branch and its head whips around one-hundred and eighty degrees. Its eyes glow yellow-green in the beam of light. Wyatt takes a big breath in and out and calms himself. *You've got this.*

Wyatt continues on and stumbles across an old dead tree that's rotted out and weathered from decades of exposure, rot, and decay. *This is perfect.* Wyatt gathers as many of the old branches in his arms as he can and struggles to hold the flashlight but he manages.

Suddenly, a flashlight beam shines on the back of Wyatt's head.

"Wyatt, what're you doing out here at this hour?" calls out a voice from the darkness behind him.

Wyatt's startled. He panics, drops the pieces of wood, spins around, and shines his beam on the man standing in front of him. Wyatt can't see the man yet because his light blinds Wyatt's eyes but it's Cheveyo Dogmoon, a Native-American forest ranger that works for the parks service. He's no spring chicken and has some grey in his hair. He has a backpack slung around his shoulder.

"Cheveyo, is that you?" asks Wyatt.

Cheveyo turns off his flashlight and Wyatt's vision clears.

"Yeah, buddy, it's me."

"Oh thank God, you scared the s-h-i-t out of me." adds Wyatt.

"Well, I hope you brought some tp then."

Wyatt laughs.

"Need a hand?"

Minutes later....

Wyatt and Cheveyo each sit on a log around a small, crackling fire. Wyatt finds the familiar scent of burning hemlock to be comforting and soothing. He watches the flames dance for a moment and Cheveyo takes note of his sullen demeanor.

"So, do you wanna talk about it?" inquires Cheveyo.

Wyatt shakes his head. Upset.

"I see... why don't we make a deal?" asks Cheveyo, reaching for the backpack at his side.

Cheveyo reaches in and pulls out a bag of marshmallows.

Wyatt's eyes light up and he thinks, *crap! That's the one thing I forget to bring. Probably didn't have any anyway. There's more food in this forest than in that grungy trailer.*

"How bout you tell me what's bothering you and I'll hand over this big bag 'a marshmallows?"

It's a tempting offer. Too tempting for Wyatt to pass up. He sighs and relents.

"Fine." says Wyatt, taking the bag from Cheveyo, pulling out a few, and cramming them in his mouth.

Cheveyo chuckles as Wyatt's swollen cheeks struggle to process the marshmallows. After a few seconds, Wyatt swallows.

"I need a stick." says Wyatt, looking around for a stick. He finds one, pokes it through three marshmallows, and hangs them over the fire.

"Hank is my problem." confesses Wyatt.

"I see… that's your mother's boyfriend, right?" asks Cheveyo.

"Yeah…. Hank the drunk. I hate him, he's a total loser. He hurts my mom and me."

This strikes a nerve in Cheveyo and beneath the surface he simmers with a quiet rage.

"I'm never going back there. I can't. I'm tired of being hurt. My mom does nothing to stop it. I wish I never had to go back."

"You do huh?"

Wyatt lifts his shirt and reveals bruising on his ribs.

"If this happened to you when you were a kid, would you want to go back?"

Cheveyo struggles to control his simmering rage. He thinks to himself, *That bastard, if only I could get my hands on him.* "No, I wouldn't," he replies.

"I'm *never* going back."

"They're going to come looking for you, Wyatt. You know that, right?" asks Cheveyo.

"Yeah, I know."

"So, what's your plan then?" inquires Cheveyo.

"I'll run, hide, even dig a tunnel if I have to and live underground." says Wyatt.

"Imagine you had the wings of an eagle or the hind legs of a mountain lion. Imagine how high and how far you could soar or how fast you could run and climb. It'd be pretty great, huh?"

"I wish. That'd be awesome. I'd never be afraid or have to worry about anything else for the rest of my life!" shouts Wyatt excitedly with a huge smile on his face.

Cheveyo smiles but there's great pain and sorrow beneath his veneer.

"Well, I should probably get going. Enjoy the marshmallows. Is there anything else you need?" asks Cheveyo with sincerity. It's clear that Cheveyo cares a great deal about Wyatt.

"Nope, I'll be fine." replies Wyatt.

"You're a good boy, Wyatt." says Cheveyo, putting a supportive hand on Wyatt's shoulder. "You take care now."

"See ya. Thanks, for stopping by." says Wyatt.

Cheveyo gets up from his log.

"Anytime."

Cheveyo walks away into the darkness and Wyatt heads inside his one-man tent. He secures the flap and crawls into his sleeping bag for a restful night's sleep.

***

Hours later, the sun rises on the Tall Oaks trailer park.

Emily wakes on the couch. The TV's still on, and she looks over at probably still drunk, Hank snoring away.

"Ugh." says Emily as she wipes the sleep from her eyes, gets up, and heads to Wyatt's bedroom. She tries the door but it won't open.

"Wyatt?" she calls out. "Wyatt, come on. Open the door please." she says knocking on the door but there's no response.

"Wyatt?!" shouts Emily, banging on the door and waking Hank.

"Whiskey's better than vodka you idiot, huh, what?" grumbles Hank as he wakes from his drunken stupor, hungover and disoriented.

"What the hell's going on?" asks Hank, his eyes squinting from the bright sunlight shining through the living room windows.

"He's not answering me and the door's locked. Something's wrong, Hank!" hollers Emily, struggling to open Wyatt's bedroom door.

"Christ, I'm sick and tired of that little shitstain, Emily. I swear to God I can't wait until he's old enough so we can kick his ass outta here! Sixteen, we can legally boot his ass outta here! Only need to put up with this shit for four more years." shouts Hank as he gets up from the couch and rushes over to the bedroom door.

"Move out of the way, Emily," grumbles Hank, shoving her out of the way.

He pounds on the door with a fist. "Open up you little freak or your ass is grass!"

Hank pounds on the door a few more times. "I've had it with this kid!" hollers Hank as he body checks the door and smashes it open, damaging the frame and hinges.

Both Emily and Hank stare at the empty bedroom and open window. "Oh, shit." says Hank.

Emily screams.

Less than fifteen minutes later, police officers are on scene with emergency lights flashing…

Sheriff Jack Ritter is on the scene. He's got a beer belly, a cowboy hat, and cowboy boots. He sweats profusely and has large pit stains under his arms.

"So, when was the last time you saw the boy, Emily? Or were you too drunk to remember?" inquires the sheriff as he gnaws on a toothpick.

"You go to hell, Jack. You know I remember you back from high school. What was that nickname the guys gave you back in high school?" asks Emily, not backing down.

The sheriff, embarrassed, looks around at his fellow officers. In towns, this small gossip spreads faster than an Indiana brush fire.

"That was back in high school," scolds the Sheriff , "You need to grow up, Emily!"

"Well, c'mon don't be shy, Jack. Go on, tell everyone what they called you. Wack-off Jack, right?! Because people caught you wackin' off all over the freakin' place ya pervert." mocks Emily.

"Okay, that's enough! Now, when was the last time you saw your son?"

"Last night, we got into an argument about Hank and he ran into his room and locked the door. That's the last we saw of him." explains Emily. "He threatened to run away."

"Any idea where he might've run off too?" asks Det. Ritter.

"That Rocky Hollow Falls forest place, no doubt. Wyatt has this forest ranger friend he meets up with sometimes. Some native guy, Chov-Chov- no, Cheveyo. Yeah, Cheveyo Dogwood or no, Dogmoon. Yeah, that's it.

Cheveyo Dogmoon." says Emily. "I'm surprised I remembered that."

"Me too," quips the Sheriff .

"I've said it before and I'll say it again. Go to hell, Jack."

***

Minutes later, an eagle soars high above the tree canopy at the Rocky Hollow Falls Canyon Nature Preserve. Its sharp eyes scan the forest floor looking for small, easy, and tasty prey.

Down below, Wyatt wakes in his tent. His hands reach up to wipe the sleep from his eyes and, to his shock and amazement, he has fury, reddish paws instead of human hands.

"Ahhh! Holy crap." shouts Wyatt as he springs up on all fours. Wyatt's a red fox. "Oh. My. God." He darts out of his tent and runs and leaps through the forest, weaving through trees. His sense of smell, hearing, and vision is heightened. He can smell and hear everything. Wyatt leaps over the trunk of a fallen tree and scampers to the edge of the Wabash river. This section of the river is very calm and tranquil. Wyatt looks down at the water and sees his reflection.

"Jesus, now I understand why mom used to tell me to be careful of what I wished for." says Wyatt, concerned, but his concern is short-lived as his heart fills with joy and excitement. "My wish came true!" shouts Wyatt, smiling at his watery reflection.

Suddenly, Wyatt hears multiple voices shouting loudly. They're calling out his name.

Dogs are barking. The commotion appears to be getting closer and louder.

It's a police and volunteer search team and they're closing in.

Wyatt thinks fast, *Oh no, I can't go back to my camp. What am I going to do?! For one thing, start by calming yourself and think, Wyatt, think. This is what you've always wanted. This is your moment. This is your time to be free.*

Wyatt engages his hind-legs, zeroes in on his best escape route, and bolts away into the forest at lighting speed.

CHAPTER 3

One with the Animals

Wyatt sits perched above a hilltop. His red, fury tail perks upright. He watches the search party look for him repeatedly call out his name.

"Wyatt! Wyatt!"

"Suckers. Little do they know I'm standing right here. They'll never find me." says Wyatt, chuckling and scratching behind his ear with a hind leg. *God, that feels good. Ooh, aah, oh yeah, I like that. That feels nice.*

Sheriff Ritter and other uniformed police officers converge on Wyatt's campsite.

Sheriff Ritter puts his hand over a small pile of smoldering embers.

"Still warm," he says. "He couldn't've gone too far."

Sheriff Ritter looks around at his officers and gives some marching orders.

"Listen up! I want an officer posted at this campsite until further notice in case he comes back. I need somebody to put a call out to the feds and get me some air support, and somebody please get a hold of the Forestry Service 'n find out about this Cheveyo Dogmoon fella. See if they've got any Native American forest rangers by that name. Okay, c'mon people, let's go let's go!" orders the Sheriff with fervor.

An hour later, a helicopter flies overhead. The pilot looks out his window and searches for any signs of Wyatt. No luck.

The search for Wyatt continues. Emily joins in the search. Hank is too busy drinking beer back at the trailer.

A uniformed police officer wraps up a conversation on his cellphone and approaches the Sheriff.

"Sheriff Ritter?" asks the young officer.

"Yeah."

"I just got off the phone with the forestry service and they've never heard of a Cheveyo Dogmoon. They searched their employment records database going back thirty years and they found nothing. I ran the name through our systems and same thing. The guy doesn't exist."

"Shit."

"D'you think this is connected to the disappearances of those other kids?" inquires the young officer.

"Christ, I don't know. Where's mom?" asks the sheriff.

"She's at the back of the pack."

The Sheriff approaches Emily at the tail end of the search line.

"Emily, can I have a word with you for a second please?" asks Sheriff Ritter.

Emily stops and faces him.

"What?"

"There's a few things I'd like to tell you, but I need you to promise me that you'll relax and not flip out, okay?" says the sheriff.

"Okay, I promise. Spit it out."

"We spoke with the Forestry Service and they've never heard of a Cheveyo Dogmoon." explains the Sheriff as Emily's eyes widen with concern.

"That's impossible. Wyatt talks about him all the time. They're friends."

"Emily, we ran his name through our police databases too. He doesn't exist." explains the sheriff as panic sets in for Emily.

"Oh my God. Wyatt was taken, wasn't he? Like those other kids that went missing from Winslow. Oh, my God!" shouts Emily, quickly breaking her promise to be calm and relax. "If the guy was using a fake name, then he must be the one who took him, right?! Oh, my God! Find my kid!"

"Emily, you promised you'd-"

"Oh, go to hell, Jack!" yells Emily, resuming her search.

***

Later, Wyatt leaps around through the forest. He's hungry and in search of food.

Within seconds, he sees something plowing its way through a thicket of green ferns.

It's a wild boar. Wyatt's nose twitches, he can smell the meat. Wyatt crouches down in an attack position and prepares to strike. He licks his lips and thinks to himself, *I could use some pork chops. I'm starving,* but the feral boar is big and intimidating, Wyatt soon realizes that as a red fox, he's outgunned and outmatched in this fight.

Suddenly, Wyatt feels something. His body shakes and convulses. "What's happening to me? Oh man."

Wyatt's morphing.

His bone density increases rapidly. His color changes, his paws grow big, his eyes are now those of a vicious predator and not a friendly fox.

Wyatt shape-shifts into a Mountain Lion.

He's a mature, male cat in his physical prime. Dangerous. Menacing.

Wyatt crouches down as low as he can and watches the chubby, dark-colored boar moving rapidly through the ferns. He's waiting for the opportune time to pounce. He hears the boar's grunts and snorts grow louder. It's getting closer.

It's time.

Wyatt leaps from the ground and soars through the air with his claws protruding out as far as possible. His jaw gapes and reveals large, razor sharp fangs.

The boar freezes with fear and stops dead in its tracks. A big mistake.

Wyatt thrashes at the boar with his claws and sinks his fangs in its neck.

The boar lets out a loud pig squeal as blood gushes from the puncture wounds in its neck. The distressing squeal is enough to spook the birds up in the forest canopy. They soar high in the sky in search of a more tranquil area where mountain lions aren't tearing boars to shreds.

A few hundred meters away, some officers searching for Wyatt get spooked too.

"What was that?" asks one of the officers drawing his weapon.

"I don't know and I don't wanna find out." replies another officer, visibly concerned.

Wyatt tears and rips at the flesh with his fangs. He enjoys his savory meal.

***

Minutes later, Wyatt lays stretched out next to the boar's carcass. His mountain lion belly is full, there's blood on his paws and smeared on his face. He burps.

Suddenly, Wyatt hears some sticks on the forest floor cracking and snapping from the east. His head whips around and within seconds he's on all fours, alert. Then, he smells it. Something unmistakable and familiar.

Humans.

An officer stumbles through a patch of tall plants and comes face to face with Wyatt.

The officer does what he's told perps to do many times in the past. He freezes. Wyatt growls and snarls loudly in an attempt at intimidating the officer. It's working.

"Oh shit, oh shit," says the officer as he hears more officers approaching from behind. "Guys, stay back, we've got a mountain lion here!" The other officers heed his warning and stop advancing.

"Good kitty cat, that's all you are. Just a kitty cat. Only bigger. A lot bigger, scarier, and way more dangerous. Oh shit, oh shit." says the officer.

Wyatt growls loudly and swings his paws and claws around wildly.

"Okay, okay. I'm just gonna back away. Real casual like, nice and easy. I'm sorry for disturbing your meal. Yeah, see, you're a friendly kitty." says the officer as he steps backward slowly.

Wyatt belts out his loudest possible growl and swings his paws again. He shows his fangs and that's about all the officer can stand. The officer turns and runs full speed away from Wyatt to his fellow officers who by now have started laughing.

"Oh yeah, real funny guys! I almost shit myself for cryin' out loud." confesses the young officer only to have his pals laugh even harder.

***

The sun sets and a bright moon rises over the town of Sugar Creek.

Back at the Tall Oaks trailer park, Emily lies on the couch in a fetal position and cries.

Hank drinks a can of beer on an old recliner chair and thinks to himself, *Jesus Christ, am I gonna have to listen to this shit all night? I'm sick of it! The little shitstain's probably laughin' at all the fuss he created anyway. Shit, I'm glad he's gone and here's to hopin' it stays that way.* Hank raises his beer can, toasts to his thoughts, and takes a big gulp. He looks over at Emily with a scornful look in his eyes.

"Are you gonna be like this all night for Christ's sake?"

Emily looks up at Hank. "Are you kidding me? My son is missing, Hank!" yells Emily.

"Oh, gimme a break, Emily. If he's missing, it's because he wants to be! Ever think that maybe he's a runner just like his momma was?" asks Hank.

"Just shut up, Hank. I don't wanna talk. It's your fault anyway that he ran away. It's because he hates you!"

"Okay, you know what, Emily? I don't have time for this shit. I'm goin' to the bar. You're bein' a real drag tonight." replies Hank as he gets up from the recliner chair and pulls his truck keys out of his pocket.

"My son is missing, you idiot! You think I feel like partyin' tonight?!" hollers Emily. "What the hell is wrong with you, Hank?!"

"Alright, I'm outta here. I'm not hearin' this shit right now." says Hank as he storms out of the trailer.

***

Minutes later, in the Rocky Hollow Falls Canyon Nature Preserve, flashlight beams move through a thick patch of hemlock trees.

"Okay, guys, that's it for tonight!" shouts Sheriff Ritter.

***

The following morning, Wyatt wakes in his mountain lion form. His paws and face are still stained with blood. The hot June sun beats down hard on the forest. It's going to be a hot one today.

He gets up and jaunts over to a stream for a drink and a quick bath. The water washes away the boar blood. Wyatt shakes himself off and beads of water fly off his fur coat.

Next, Wyatt's on the prowl and sniffing. He's desperately searching for something. What could it be? Suddenly, he finds it! Excited, he spins around a few times. It's a very special place. The perfect kind of place to...

...Take a poo.

Roughly a mile away at the main entrance to the preserve, police officers, volunteers, and search dogs prepare for day two of searching for Wyatt.

They gather supplies, materials, and allow the bloodhounds to sniff items of Wyatt's clothing so that they can hopefully, pick up and track his scent.

Sheriff Ritter gives the day's marching orders.

"Okay guys, listen up! You've got your maps with your designated team zones. Remember to always stay in pairs of two. If your team finds something, the officer with the air horn sounds off for a few seconds. That way, the rest of us can come and assist. Does everyone understand?"

Some officers nod yes.

"Any questions?" asks the Sheriff.

There aren't any.

"Alright then. Remember, it's going to be as hot as a bison's ball sack out here today, so stay hydrated. I don't need any a you guys passin' out on me. If your team needs water, put a request out over the radio and command HQ will arrange for water runners to bring water to your location. They've got ATV's so they'll get there fast. Safety first. So you're aware, we've received a number of reports from locals about a big black bear roamin' around. Now, I haven't seen him yet personally, but the locals call him Big Ben, like that clock. Apparently, Big Ben's hungrier and grumpier than your average bear. He broke into a few trailers and cottages last week, tore the places up, and raided their fridges. So, if you see him, be on your guard and act accordingly. Okay, come on guys, let's go!"

The teams disperse and fan out across the forest.

Nearly a mile away, Wyatt's all done his business and thinks to himself, *I feel so much better now.*

He prances through a clearing in search of something, anything at all.

He's never felt so free, safe, and secure in his entire life. He darts across the clearing as fast as he can, leaping periodically into the air. *This is so cool!* He thinks. *I can do anything! There's no one to answer to or bother! Especially Hank! If he ever came near me, I'd tear him to pieces in two seconds!*

"I'm the master of this forest." asserts Wyatt, leaping into the air growling and snarling excitedly. "I'm the forest king!"

"No, you're not. You're just a dork." calls out a young woman's voice of similar age.

She startles Wyatt and he thinks, *What the hell?!* as he flinches and spins around.

Standing there is a beautiful bobcat, beautiful enough to take Wyatt's breath away and make his heart skip a beat.

CHAPTER 4

Never Going Back

Wyatt stands proud in his Mountain Lion form. He admires the attractive female bobcat and the myriad of dark spots covering her face and body.

"What are you?" asks Wyatt, completely enamored by her beauty.

"Isn't it obvious? I'm a bobcat. Don't you know your animals?"

"Um, yeah, yeah, I do but…" says Wyatt with his brain malfunctioning, because all he can think is *Gosh, she's beautiful. Snap out of it, Wyatt. She'll think you're an idiot.*

"But what? Hellooo?" she says wondering why Wyatt's brain isn't engaged.

"Uh, never mind..." he replies. "So, anyway, you can talk." remarks Wyatt chuckling.

"Oh, wow look at you, you're very observant." she says sarcastically with a bit of an attitude. "I'm Jenny, nice to meet you."

"I'm Wyatt, nice meeting you."

"So, you're the reason the forest has been crawling with cops and volunteers for the last few days." says Jenny. "I could hear them calling out your name. So, like, do you wanna go for a run or something?" asks Jenny.

"Sure, that'd be awesome. Let's do it." Wyatt says, smiling brightly. "Lead the way."

Jenny darts off. Her hind legs propel her forward at astonishing speeds.

"Holy crud!" shouts Wyatt, he wasn't expecting that from his smaller feline companion.

Wyatt takes off rapidly and struggles to catch up to Jenny. He pushes himself, runs at full speed, and eventually closes the gap.

Jenny dashes over a set of downed trees, through a patch of bushes, and finally comes to a stop at the top of a moss covered cliff face, overlooking the entire forest.

A small waterfall pours into the Wabash river several feet below.

Wyatt is winded and struggles to catch his breath. Jenny's fine. She's done this many times before.

"You gonna be alright?" asks Jenny, chuckling.

"Yeah, I'll be fine. I just need a-" Wyatt falls over and lays on a big slab of moss covered rock.

"Break" says Wyatt.

Jenny laughs. It's clear the pair have an instant connection.

Meanwhile, the search continues for Wyatt miles away.

Sheriff Ritter and his men call out his name. "Wyatt?! Wyatt?!"

The bloodhounds appear confused and are unable to track Wyatt's scent.

"Damnit, where is this kid? If he's missin' it's probly cuz he wants to be. Prob'ly figures it's better bein' out here than back home at that trailer with those drunks. Can't say I blame him."

****

Back at the Tall Oaks Trailer Park, Emily sits at a picnic table outside the trailer. She sips a beer and appears stressed like she hasn't slept.

Hank's pick-up truck pulls up and Emily's not happy. He's been out all night and he's just getting home at around 9:30 AM. Emily thinks to herself, *He's a low down cheatin' dog.*

Emily approaches the driver's side window and the smell of women's perfume fills Emily's nostrils.

"Hey, baby," says Hank with a drunken look on his face.

Emily doesn't say a word. She starts slapping Hank about the head and face repeatedly.

"What the hell, baby?!" shouts Hank attempting to shield his head and face.

Some residents of the trailer park are outside and gawk. None are surprised.

"You show up here, smellin' like a whore house, get outta here! We're done, Hank! Wyatt was right! I deserve so much better than you! Get the hell outta here!" shouts Emily, getting in a few more slaps to Hank's face.

"Screw you, you crazy bitch! I don't need this shit! You're a lousy lay anway!" shouts Hank as he starts the ignition, puts his truck in reverse, and peels out of the trailer park.

Emily screams and throws an almost full can of beer at the rear window of Hank's pick-up truck. Spider cracks spread through the glass.

61

***

Back at the mossy cliff face, Jenny and Wyatt lay side by side and take in the magnificent view overlooking the sixteen-hundred acre preserve.

"It's incredible, isn't it?" asks Jenny with a smile.

"Amazing." replies Wyatt. "Hey, can I ask you something?"

"Shoot."

"What happened to us? I mean I'm not complaining, I love my new life, but I need to know how all of this is possible." explains Wyatt.

Jenny stares at Wyatt for a moment.

"What?" he asks.

"I was wondering how long it'd take you to ask me that. Most people ask me right away."

responds Jenny. "But, to be honest I don't think it's my place to explain the whole thing. You should really talk to the one who made it all happen."

"God?" asks Wyatt.

"No, not God silly." replies Jenny chuckling.

Suddenly, something dawns on Wyatt. Lightbulb.

"Cheveyo…"

Jenny nods and purrs.

"I haven't seen him around." adds Wyatt.

"Trust me, he's around. He's always around." replies Jenny.

"Wait, why are you here?" asks Wyatt.

Jenny hesitates at first. It isn't an easy question to answer. It's like peeling a fresh scab off of a wound.

"My mom divorced my dad and moved to Canada to start a new life. I was mad at her at first for breaking up our family, so I decided to stay with my dad. Then, I soon realized why she left him and needed to get as far away as possible. After she left, my dad took my cell phone away and wouldn't let me talk to her. Not long after that, he started beating me and doing other things to me too." confesses Jenny.

"Jesus, Jenny, I'm really sorry."

"It's okay, I've never been happier. I really miss my mom, though. Sometimes, I think about running to Canada and trying to find her, but I don't think I'd make it that far. It's a real shame because I miss her so much and would love to see her again, but I don't want to go back to the old me. I'm happy with the way things are. I'm never going back."

"How old are you?" inquires Wyatt.

Jenny's head perks up.

"Don't you know you're never supposed to ask a woman that?" quips Jenny, smirking.

"Oh, I'm sorry."

"Relax, I'm only teasing. I'm thirteen." says Jenny.

"A year older than me." replies Wyatt. "I'm here for the same reason too. My mom's boyfriend is the biggest jerk in the world. He hurts us. He's violent."

***

Hours later, the sun sets on the Rocky Hollow Falls Canyon Nature Preserve and Sheriff Ritter sends his men home for the day.

Meanwhile, back at the trailer park, Emily lays on the couch in the living room, crying.

Sheriff Ritter's police cruiser pulls up to Emily's trailer. He steps out of the vehicle, approaches the front door, and knocks.

The door opens and Emily stands in the doorway visibly upset.

"Any luck?" says Emily wiping tears.

"Nothing yet, Emily. I had an officer staked out inside Wyatt's tent all night just in case he came back and he didn't. We'll keep looking." explains Sheriff Ritter.

"Yeah, for how long? How long did you guys look for all those other kids that're still missin'?" asks Emily.

"Emily, I know you're upset but try to have a little faith, okay." says the Sheriff.

A tearful Emily nods yes, "Okay."

Sheriff Ritter gets back in his cruiser and drives out of the trailer park. Emily heads back inside the trailer.

Nearby, in a thicket of brush, Wyatt and Jenny are crouched down and watching.

"Your mom's really sad." says Jenny.

They watch Emily through the living room windows. She lays back down on the couch and cries.

"I know."

They see a blue pick-up truck pull up to the trailer and hit a few garbage cans.

"Who's that?" asks Jenny.

The commotion startles Emily and they see her get up from the couch and head for the front door.

"That's him. Hank. The reason I ran away. That's the jerk."

They watch as Hank stumbles out of his pick-up truck and staggers toward the trailer.

Inside the trailer, Emily locks the front door.

Hank bangs on the trailer door and hollers, "Emily, let me in. Let me in you stupid bitch!

"Go back to your whore!" yells Emily.

Wyatt and Jenny observe from the thicket of brush.

"See what I mean?" asks Wyatt.

Hank kicks the door repeatedly and within seconds, he's inside.

"Bastard." adds Jenny.

Emily runs to her bedroom.

"Get back here, you bitch!" shouts Hank as he chases Emily into the bedroom.

Hank throws Emily down onto the bed and back hands her a few times across the face.

"You ever disrespect me like that again in public and I'll kill you!" Hank strikes Emily a few more times and causes her nose to bleed. "Stone cold dead! You hear me, bitch?!"

"Let that be a lesson to ya!" yells Hank, storming out of the room and heading for the fridge. He opens the door to the fridge and there's a little blood on the back of his hand. He takes all the cans of beer and heads back out to his pick-up, staggering.

Hank approaches the truck and hops inside. He sticks his key in the ignition and starts the engine, but Hank senses that something isn't quite right. He looks in his rearview mirror and sees a mountain lion sitting upright in his back seat, staring at him. It's Wyatt.

"Oh, shit."

Wyatt growls and roars as fiercely as he can.

Hank freaks out, whips open his driver's side door to make a run for it, but Jenny's there, growling and thrashing at him with her paws and claws.

Hank is viciously attacked by Wyatt and Jenny.

Wyatt bites Hank on the back of the neck, sinks his fangs into him, and pulls him back into the truck.

Hank screams and his eyes are wide with terror as he's mercilessly mauled.

Some of the lights inside nearby trailers illuminate.

Jenny hops into the truck and joins Wyatt for the drunken-asshole buffet.

Within seconds, Jenny and Wyatt, have clawed, bitten, and ripped Hank to shreds. One of his eyeballs dangles from it's socket.

Hank's as dead as a petrified piece of hemlock tree floating down the Wabash.

***

A short while later, police vehicles, an ambulance, and a van from the coroner's office are on scene. Sheriff Ritter steps out of his cruiser and approaches Hank's pick-up to take a peek inside.

Crime scene techs snap photos of Hank and his truck. Well, what's left of Hank.

Emily sits on the steps of her porch. A young paramedic treats the wounds on her face. Emily looks at him and thinks, *not bad, kinda cute.* Apparently, she isn't too bothered by the fact that Hank's been torn to pieces.

"Jesus H. Christ," says the sheriff, looking inside the pick-up truck. A deputy approaches "So, what d'you think, sheriff? Closed casket?" asks the deputy jokingly.

"I'm thinking more like a closed shoe box." replies the Sheriff.

"Anybody notify his next of kin?" asks the Sheriff.

"I'm on it." says the deputy.

"Thanks, Billy," says the Sheriff, turning his attention to Emily. Despite their frosty relationship, he feels sorry for Emily and all that she's going through. He approaches Emily with a smile.

"Emily, I want you to know that if Hank wasn't torn to pieces by what I suspect was one, maybe even two now that I come to think of it, very pissed off mountain lions, I'd be putting him in a jail cell tonight for what he did to you. That ain't right and… I'm sorry that happened to you." admits the Sheriff.

Emily nods and lights a cigarette.

"Thanks, Jack."

"Tomorrow morning, we're headin' out to the preserve first thing to look for Wyatt. On top of that, we've gotta track two mountain lions and take them down. I understand it's their natural instinct to eat and all, but we can't have 'em eatin' the residents of Tall Oaks even if they are wife-beating drunks."

Emily nods and puffs on her cigarette energetically.

"Take care of yourself, Emily. You should really quit those." advises the sheriff.

"Should quit wife beaters and guys that treat me and my kid like shit too." replies Emily.

"Damn right you should. I know you're worth more than that, Emily." asserts Sheriff Ritter. "The question is, do you?"

"Please, find my son, I need my son. I'd rather be dead than live without my son. Did you guys ever find those missing kids from Winslow, Jack?"

He hesitates to tell her the unfortunate truth and shakes his head, no.

"The feds are on the case and we're working all the angles, Emily. To be perfectly honest, there's no evidence that anything bad ever happened to those kids. A lot of us feel that they're missin' because they wanna be. They all came from homes that some might consider to be, broken homes, I guess would be the best way to describe it."

"Yeah, homes like this one." says Emily, clinically depressed. Jack thinks to himself, *Christ, you're an idiot, Jack.*

"I never said that, Emily."

Emily cries. "You don't have to. I know."

CHAPTER 5

The Lost Children

Dawn breaks on the preserve. Rays of light pierce the canopy and warm the forest floor. It's only 6AM and already, the preserve feels like a sauna.

Jenny and Wyatt wash the blood from their faces and cool off in a nearby stream.

Jenny splashes water playfully into Wyatt's face. He laughs and responds by doing the same to her. They're flirting.

Jenny thinks, *He's cute. I wanna kiss him, but he should be the one making the first move. Not me, he's the man. Ugh, maybe I'm being too old-fashioned.*

Wyatt thinks to himself, *kiss her you idiot, she's into you. Just do it! Wait, what if she slaps me?*

"Oh, to heck with it," says Jenny.

"Screw it. If I get slapped it'll be worth it." says Wyatt, making a move at the same time as Jenny.

The young lovebirds share their first kiss. It's a poignant moment.

Suddenly, the sounds of barking bloodhounds disrupts their romantic peace and solitude. Their noses twitch and they smell a familiar scent.

Humans.

Sheriff Ritter stumbles down an embankment to the river with officers in toe. He spots Wyatt and Jenny. "There!"

Officers open fire and take shots at the wild cats.

Wyatt growls angrily. He and Jenny dart away as fast as they can, leaping across the stream and heading into a patch of tall grasses.

Sheriff Ritter and the officers follow in hot pursuit, still firing.

The officers plow through the tall grasses swatting the vegetation away as best they can so they're able to see in front of them. Finally, they emerge into a clearing and see Wyatt and Jenny darting away.

"Fire!" shouts Sheriff Ritter as the officers take aim, discharge their weapons, and send a volley of hot lead toward Wyatt and Jenny.

Suddenly, the officers hear a thunderous *ROAR!* They stop and take note.

"Jesus, what the hell was that?!" yells one of the officers.

For the majority of the officers, it's a sound they've never heard before and one they'll never forget.

The officers hear loud thuds. They turn and look at the patch of head-height tall grass behind them. The big blades of grass rustle and shake. Something's displacing them rapidly.

Whatever it is, it's heading straight for them and fast.

A large and furious, adult male black bear emerges from the patch and charges straight for the officers.

"Shit! Big Ben!" screams the Sheriff as officers take aim but it's too late. The bear is already on top of the Sheriff, biting and tearing at his trigger arm.

The Sheriff screams in pain. Officers hesitate to fire out of fear of hitting the Sheriff.

Within seconds, the sheriff's arm looks as though it's gone twelve rounds with a garbage disposal.

One of the officers decides to take a shot with his pump shotgun. He quickly determines the best place to shoot Big Ben is right in the ass.

The officer takes aim, pulls the trigger, and a wad of buckshot blows a gaping hole in Big Ben's ass. He lets go of the sheriff's arm and cries out in pain.

Birds in the forest canopy above panic and take flight in search of a more tranquil location.

Meanwhile, nearly half a mile away, Wyatt and Jenny stop and turn.

"Oh no!" says Jenny, deeply concerned. "Ben!"

Jenny darts off toward the bear's cry, leaving Wyatt behind.

"Jenny! No!" shouts Wyatt taking off after her back through the forest.

Big Ben runs away from the officers at full speed. The officers quickly take aim and fire their weapons until they run out of ammunition.

Big Ben runs down a popular hiking trail past some terrified hikers who run out of the way, screaming.

Jenny runs fast, leaping over downed trees with Wyatt hot on her hind heels.

She spots Big Ben and calls out to him. "Ben! This way!"

The wounded black bear sees Jenny and bolts toward her as fast as he can.

Jenny runs and guides Big Ben to a safe and secluded area.

***

Minutes later, Big Ben lays on his side bleeding out in a hidden clearing of ferns. Wyatt and Jenny stand next to him on all fours, gravely concerned. Jenny cries.

"You saved our butts back there. Thank you." says Wyatt.

"No sweat, you're welcome. All it took was me getting shot in mine." replies Big Ben.

"Stop your crying." instructs Big Ben, looking at Jenny. "Everything's gonna be alright. Watch this."

Suddenly, Big Ben trembles, convulses, and morphs into human form.

Wyatt can't believe his eyes. He's never seen anything morph and shape-shift before.

As Big Ben transitions, a familiar face comes into view.

"Cheveyo..." whispers Wyatt, his eyes widening in astonishment.

"Why didn't you tell me?" Wyatt asks, looking at Jenny.

"Because it wasn't my place to tell you his story." replies Jenny, as Cheveyo transitions into a fully formed, uninjured human man, dressed like a forest ranger.

"Howdy, buddy," says Cheveyo, smiling brightly at Wyatt.

Wyatt runs up to Cheveyo, stands on his hind legs, gives him a hug, and licks him all over the face.

"Okay, okay settle down!" Cheveyo says, laughing. "You're slobbering all over my face."

Wyatt settles down on all fours.

"How is all of this possible? How're we able to morph like this? Please Cheveyo, I need to know! Is it just us, or are there others?!" asks Wyatt, unable to contain his excitement.

Cheveyo chuckles, "You're full of questions, aren't ya? Why don't I start by answering the last question first."

Cheveyo trembles, shakes, and shape-shifts into a large, coyote.

"Cool," says Wyatt, amazed.

Cheveyo tilts his head up high to the sky and howls as loud as he can with everything he's got.

Meanwhile, a half-mile away, Sheriff Ritter is loaded onto a stretcher. What's left of his arm is bandaged tightly. It looks like a football made of gauze. Paramedics, police officers, and the Sheriff hear Cheveyo's call to the animal kingdom. They stop and look in the direction of the call.

Without warning, dozens of deer emerge from the forest and dart past the officers.

"Holy shit!" shouts one of the officers as he and others take cover. A big buck slams hard into the Sheriff's stretcher, and sends him hurling to the ground.

Foxes spring out from a patch of hydrangeas and leap past the officers.

Badgers, muskrats, and chipmunks leap out of the forest from multiple directions and zip by the officers.

Snakes crawl out of the depths of the forest floor past the officers next.

"Oh, my God." remarks one of the officers as he and his colleagues observe the never-before-seen wildlife spectacle in awe.

***

Minutes later, back at the patch of ferns, hundreds of animals from the Rocky Hollow

Falls Canyon kingdom gather round Cheveyo, Wyatt, and Jenny.

Wyatt can't believe his eyes. He's shocked to his core. "Incredible."

Wyatt looks at Cheveyo and smiles.

"That's nothing. Check this out,' says Cheveyo.

All of the animals tremble, shake, and morph into their human forms. They're all child and teenage boys and girls. All of them smile and wave to Wyatt.

"I can't believe it, you guys are the kids from the news." says Wyatt.

Wyatt looks down at his paws but sees his human hands. He's in human form like everyone else.

Wyatt looks at Jenny and she too is in human form. He's captivated by her long, beautiful brunette hair, hazel eyes, and ivory skin. Jenny smiles bright. "Hey."

"Hey." replies Wyatt in utter disbelief. "You're so beautiful"

Some of the children giggle at the remark.

"Thanks," says Jenny, chuckling. "You're not so bad yourself, dork." She gives him a peck on the cheek.

Cheveyo chimes in and talks to Wyatt. "Now, let me answer your first and second question, Wyatt. When I was a small boy, I was a member of the Pawdi tribe. I lived with my mother and father in a small cabin in these very woods. It's always been the way of my people to live off the land, but like many of the children standing here before you, my father was a bad man. Actually, I can't even call him a man. He was a beast. One night, he was drunk and hurting my mother. I tried to protect her, so I hit him, but I was only ten so all it did was make him mad. He took a knife, stabbed me, and I died as a result. My spirit lifted out of my body, and I lived among the forest with the animals."

"I'm so sorry." replies Wyatt. "That's so sad."

"My spirit took the form of a black bear. One day, when my father was fishing by a creek bed all by himself, I paid him a visit. After that, I knew my mother would be safe forever. All of the children that you see here ran away to this forest because they were in the same situation as you, Wyatt. My spirit gives them the power to shape shift and hide. After my father killed me, I vowed that I would protect all children, so that what happened to me would never happen to them."

Wyatt looked around at all the safe and happy children. He'd never been so happy. Jenny took Wyatt by the hand and smiled as she too looked at all of the lost children. Wyatt has never felt so happy and safe in his entire life. Despite the overwhelmingly positive feelings, Wyatt can't help but think about his mother Emily back at Tall Oaks. *I miss her so much. I hope she's not sad and crying all the time.* He suddenly feels bad and needs to ask Cheveyo something.

"Is it possible for us to go back to the real world?" asks Wyatt.

"That's not so simple, Wyatt. Once a wish like the one you made is granted, it's impossible to reverse it. To be honest, nobody's ever asked me that because no one's ever wanted to go back."

Wyatt looks at all the children and Jenny.

"Ever?" asks Wyatt.

"Never." assures Cheveyo. "There might be a way but I definitely can't make any promises to you, Wyatt. I'm sorry."

Made in the USA
Columbia, SC
01 November 2023

24992359R00059